THE LATKE WHO COULDN'T STOP SCREAMING

M^CSWEENEY'S BOOKS
SAN FRANCISCO

For more information about McSweeney's, see www.mcsweeneys.net

ISBN: 1-932416-87-0
ISBN-13: 978-1-932416-87-9

THE

LATKE

WHO COULDN'T STOP SCREAMING

a christmas story

BY

LEMONY SNICKET

ILLUSTRATIONS BY LISA BROWN

THIS STORY ENDS IN SOMEONE'S MOUTH, BUT IT BEGINS in a tiny village more or less covered in snow. The snow had fallen during the long night, during which children had pressed their faces to the windows looking for a glimpse of a man who they suspected of bringing them wonderful gifts, but instead they heard a terrible noise from a certain cottage in the neighboring arrondissement, a word which here means "place where something was being born."

THIS COTTAGE was already regarded with some suspicion, as it was the only place not decorated with flashing colored lights at this time of year.

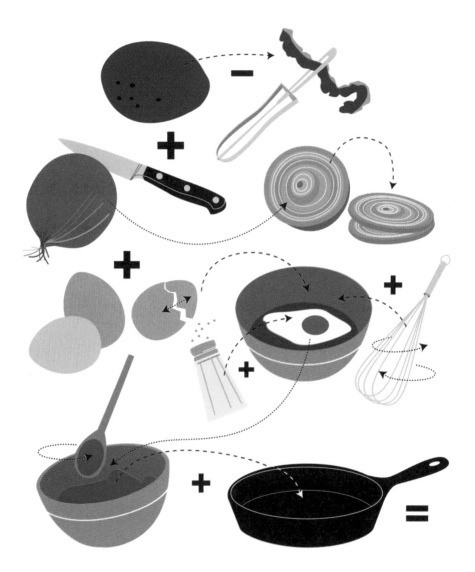

THE THING that was being born was a latke, a word which here means "potato pancake." Latkes are a traditional part of the celebration of Hanukah, a holiday commemorating a miraculous Jewish military victory. Nearly everything in this world is born screaming, and the latke was no exception, even though the latke wasn't conceived and born the way you and I were conceived and born, but instead was fashioned from grated potatoes, chopped onion, beaten eggs, and a dash or two of salt. Once these ingredients were properly mixed, the latke was slapped into a pan full of olive oil heated to a very high temperature, and this is when it began to scream.

"AAAHHHHHHHH!!!"

"AAAHHHHHHHH!!!"

THE LATKE was suffering so much that it leapt out of the hot pan and out the window of the cottage, and began to run screaming down the boulevard.

"AAAHHHHHHHHH!!!"

THIS MAY SEEM like unusual behavior for a potato pancake, but this is a Christmas story, in which things tend to happen that would never occur in real life.

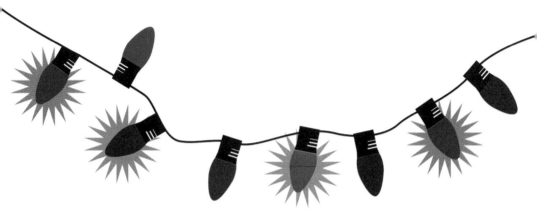

THE LATKE ran past a row of flashing colored lights, which hung from the rain gutters of a less suspicious cottage. "What's all the ruckus?" said the lights in unison. "We're the ones who are supposed to be dominating the neighborhood with our cheerful glow!"

"I was just thrown into a pan of boiling oil!" the latke cried in reply. "Can you believe it?"

"Yes," said the flashing colored lights, "but we can't imagine why."

"Because I'm a latke," said the latke. "The olive oil reminds us of the oil used to rededicate the temple following the defeat of Antiochus at the hands of the Maccabees. The oil was only supposed to last for one night but there was a miracle and it lasted for eight. Plus, frying makes my skin crispy and brown."

"SO YOU'RE BASICALLY hash browns," said the flashing colored lights. "Maybe you can be served alongside a Christmas ham."

"I'm not hash browns!" cried the latke. "I'm something completely different!"

"AAAHHHHHHHH!!!"

"AAAHHHHHHHHH!!!"

THE LATKE rounded the corner and found itself face to face with a candy cane, which wrinkled its red-and-white nose at the latke in distaste.

"I'm trying to sprinkle the night air with my peppermint scent," the candy cane said. "Your mouthwatering smell, not to mention all that yelping, is spoiling the effect."

"My mouthwatering smell is part of the cozy feeling of Hanukah," the latke replied. "It reminds us that things are better now than they were in 175 BCE, when my people were not allowed to practice their religion. In order to study the Torah they had to hide out in caves, and when they heard Greek soldiers approach they pretended they were gambling with a small, spinning top called a dreidel."

"Sort of like Joseph and Mary hiding out in the manger," said the candy cane. "Someone should write a Christmas carol about you."

"I'm not part of Christmas!" cried the latke. "It's a totally different thing!"

"AAAHHHHHHHH!!!"

"AAAHHHHHHHHH!!!"

THE SCREAMS of the latke grew quieter and quieter as the pancake ran out of the village into the surrounding forest. Its utter fury was unabated—a phrase which here means "The latke was still very annoyed at the objects to whom it had spoken"—but it was quite tired, and so it decided to rest for a few minutes beneath the branches of a little pine tree. The pine tree was napping, but woke up at the sound of an object plopping down at its feet.

"ARE YOU A present?" the pine tree asked. "Presents are pretty much the only thing allowed to sit beneath me during this time of year."

The latke sighed. "Presents aren't really a big part of Hanukah," it said in a voice hoarse from screaming. "There's nothing wrong with giving gifts to loved ones, of course, but it's more important to light the candles for eight consecutive nights, to commemorate the miracle in the temple and the miracle of victory even when you are thoroughly outnumbered, so you shouldn't give up hope."

"Plus, Santa Claus," said the pine tree.

The latke was too exhausted to scream.

"Santa Claus has nothing to do with it," the latke said. "Christmas and Hanukah are completely different things."

"But different things can often blend together," said the pine tree. "Let me tell you a funny story about pagan rituals."

But before the pine tree could begin its story, a family came trooping through the snow, searching the forest carefully.

"WE SHOULDN'T have waited until the last minute to get ready for the holiday," said the father in the family, who was holding an axe. "We'll never find a good one."

"You shouldn't give up hope," said the mother, and pointed at the pine tree. "Look!"

"It's perfect," said the daughter.

"Beautiful," agreed the son.

"Such a marvelous shape," said the mother.

"And its skin looks so crispy," said the father, and reached down and scooped up the latke from the snow. "We'll need to reheat it, of course, but this will be perfect for Hanukah dinner, with a topping of applesauce, sour cream, or even jam."

"I'll refry it in oil," said the mother, "to remind us of the rededication of the temple."

"And the triumph of the Maccabees over Antiochus," added the daughter.

"After hiding in caves all that time," the son chimed in.

THE FATHER SMILED down at the latke in his mitten, and then stared curiously at his other hand. "What was I thinking, bringing this axe?" he said to himself.

THE FAMILY STROLLED back to the village, walking past all the cottages with flashing colored lights and smiling politely at the candy canes until they reached their own home. The family carried the latke into their own home, which was warm and cozy, and sat down at the table, which was lit with the flickering candles of a menorah, or hanukkiyah, which is a branched candelabra designed specifically for the holiday.

IT IS VERY frustrating not to be understood in this world. If you say one thing and keep being told that you mean something else, it can make you want to scream. But somewhere in the world there is a place for all of us, whether you are an electric form of decoration, peppermint-scented sweet, a source of timber, or a potato pancake. On a cold, snowy night, everyone and everything should be welcomed somewhere, and the latke was welcomed into a home full of people who understood what a latke is, and how it fits into its particular holiday.

And then they ate it.

"AAA—"

LEMONY SNICKET is the author of a number of unpleasant books, including *The Miserable Mill, Horseradish,* and *The Baby In The Manger*.

LISA BROWN is the writer and illustrator of the *Baby Be of Use* books, a series of board books for busy parents, and *How to Be,* an instructional picture book for children.